ANNE F...

The Killer Cat's Birthday Bash

Illustrated by Steve Cox

PUFFIN

PUFFIN BOOKS

Pe ... 4, USA
Penguin Gr ... (Canada), 40 ... anada M4P 2Y3
Canada Inc.)

Penguin ... n Books Ltd)
Pengu ... Australia

Penguin Bo ... 110 017, India
Pe ... Zealand

Penguin Books ... 2196, South Africa

P ... ngland

puffinbooks.com

First published 2008
This edition published 2009
4

Set in Baskerville
Typeset by Palimpsest Book Production Limited, Grangemouth, Stirlingshire

Made and printed in England by Clays Ltd, St Ives plc

British Library Cataloguing in Publication Data
A CIP catalogue record for this book is available from the British Library

ISBN: 978–0–141–32436–4

www.greenpenguin.co.uk

Contents

1: Not my fault

OKAY, OKAY. SO spank my furry little
bum. I held a party.

And, go ahead. Stuff me with sorry
pills. It all ended up a bit of a mess.

Well, more than a mess. A disaster.

Well, more than a disaster. A real riot.

But it was *not my fault*. If Ellie hadn't
got so bored she rooted through the
cupboard and found that old
photograph album, I would never have
known the date of my birthday. None
of it would have happened.

So you blame Ellie. Don't blame me.

I

2: 'You talkin' 'bout me?'

IT WAS A horrible day. Horrible. The rain was splattering against the window panes. The wind was howling. So Ellie lay face down on the rug and flicked over the pages of the album.

'Oooh, Dad! Here's one of you the day you tumbled in that muddy ditch.'

(Best place for the man, if you want my opinion.)

'Oooh, Mum! Come and look at this photo. Your hair looks *lovely.*'

(On Planet No-Style, maybe. But not here.)

On and on Ellie went, squealing away

3

like that baby mouse Tiger and I gave
such a good fright behind the wheelie
bin. In the end I decided I couldn't
stand it any more, and made for the
door.

Just then she squealed again. 'Oh,

4

here's one of Tuffy! Doesn't he look *sweeeeeeeet*?'

I turned to give her one of my 'you talkin' 'bout me?' looks. She didn't even notice. She was too busy ooh-ing and aah-ing and fussing and cooing. 'Oh,

come and look at this, Mum. Tuffy looks so *cute*!'

I'm not going to hang my head in shame and make excuses for myself. Back then I was a ball of fluff. I was a *kitten*. Baby kittens *are* sweet.

Ellie picked out another photo. 'Oh, look! Tuffy is *gorgeous*!'

I couldn't help it; I was curious. So I strolled back to take a look. And sure enough, there was this photo of me, all huge and trusting eyes, and fur around me like a fluffy cloud. I looked like something off one of those soppy birthday cards your great-aunt sends to your mother.

I nearly threw up. But Ellie was pointing to the writing underneath the photo as she read it aloud.

'*Our enchanting new kitten. Born on 31st October.*'

She looked at her mother. 'It's October now,' she said. 'That means it's nearly Tuffy's birthday.'

'That's nice,' said Ellie's mother.

I thought so too. But Ellie's father had to introduce a sour note into this warm family moment.

'31st October?' he said. 'Isn't that Halloween? The time when everything evil and ugly and dangerous crawls out to stalk the land.' He snorted. 'A very suitable day indeed for Tuffy's birthday!'

Rude man. But did I bother to give him the blink? No. I was too busy thinking.

31st October. My birthday, eh?

Then why not hold a party?

Well, why not?

3: No dogs

'RIGHT,' BELLA SAID. 'First we must decide
on where we're holding this birthday bash
of yours.'

'My house, of course,' I told them.
'It's my birthday and my party, so we'll
have it at my house.'

Bella sighed. 'Have you forgotten
what day it's going to be?'

'No,' I said, and couldn't help turning
sarcastic. 'Unless I just happened to
step out tonight without my *brain*, it's
on 31st October.'

'That's right,' said Bella. 'And that's
the night your family plans to hold a

9

big Halloween party for everyone on
the street.'

'Really?' I was astonished. 'News to
me.' I turned to Tiger. 'Did you know
that?'

'Sure I knew,' Tiger told me. 'This

morning I was just sitting minding my own business on the front door mat when the invitation came through the letter box and fell on my head.' He ran a paw over his fur. 'I can still feel the lump.'

'I knew too,' Snowball told me. 'My
family have already fetched their
dressing-up box down from the attic.'
She scowled. 'And Tanya thought it
would be amusing to put a bonnet on
me.'

'What did you do?' asked Tiger.

'Scratched her, of course,' said Snowball. 'Really hard. She won't try that again.'

Everyone chuckled, except for me. I wasn't in the mood.

'I don't believe it!' I grumbled. 'You live in a house for years. They feed you, try to cuddle you and make you think that you're a member of the family. And then they send party invitations all round the town without even mentioning it in front of you!'

Bella could tell my feelings had been hurt. 'Perhaps you simply weren't around to hear them talking about it,' she suggested soothingly.

I thought back over the week. It's true I had spent most of every day out scaring squirrels. And every evening out with the gang. In fact, when I

thought about it, I'd only stepped
inside to see what sort of grub they'd
put in my dish before deciding whether

I'd rather stroll down to the fish shop
and knock the lid off their waste bin.

But still, I felt a bit sore. If my own family had decided to hold a party, you would have thought they might choose to celebrate my birthday, not stupid Halloween.

No. I was miffed enough to take a
stand.

'Right, then,' I said. 'We'll have my
party somewhere else. How about
round the recycling bins?'

'Bit dangerous,' warned Bella. 'All
those cars backing up in the dark to
dump their papers and bottles.'

17

'Under the scout hut?'

'You're joking,' Tiger said. 'It's really hard to squeeze in through that hole, and then it's freezing.'

So that settled it.

'All right,' I told them. 'We'll hold my birthday bash in the Fletchers' barn.'

'That means we'll have to invite the horses too.'

Everyone groaned. Horses. Just think about them. Cloppy great feet. Giant black nostrils you could climb up inside and then get lost. Legs as knobbly as

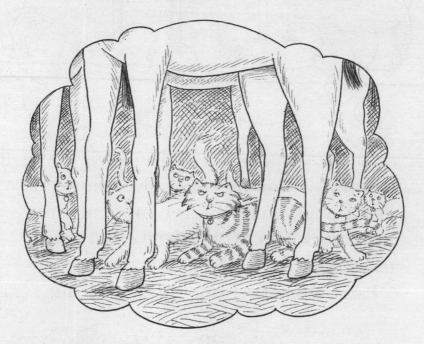

Granny's furniture. Basically, a horse is just a huge pudgy barrel on great long matchstick legs, with feet like upturned teacups.

Party animals? I don't think so! But

you can't hold a party in someone else's home, and not invite them.

'Okay, then. Horses it is.'

'What about dogs?' asked Bella.

We all turned to stare.

'Dogs?' Tiger said, and shuddered. (He'd only just got down from the last tree young Buster had chased him up.) 'No. Absolutely not.'

Snowball is more of a softie. 'Not even that harmless little thing from

Laurel Way that looks like a tiny toilet brush on legs, and is so soppy it can't even jump off a bed?'

'No,' Tiger said. 'Not even that one. If any dogs are invited, I'm not coming.'

So that was settled, then. No dogs.

4: Ghosts in the closet

ON THE WAY home, I hatched a little plan to pay my family back.

More fond of ghoulies and ghosties than of their own pussy cat, were they?

Well, I'd show them.

I sidled through the back door, then up the stairs and into Ellie's bedroom. Little Miss Goody-Two-Shoes was sitting up in bed, reading a book.

I jumped up beside her and snuggled.

'Oooh, Tuffy!' she said. 'You are so nice and sweet and cuddly.'

I kept my temper. It nearly choked

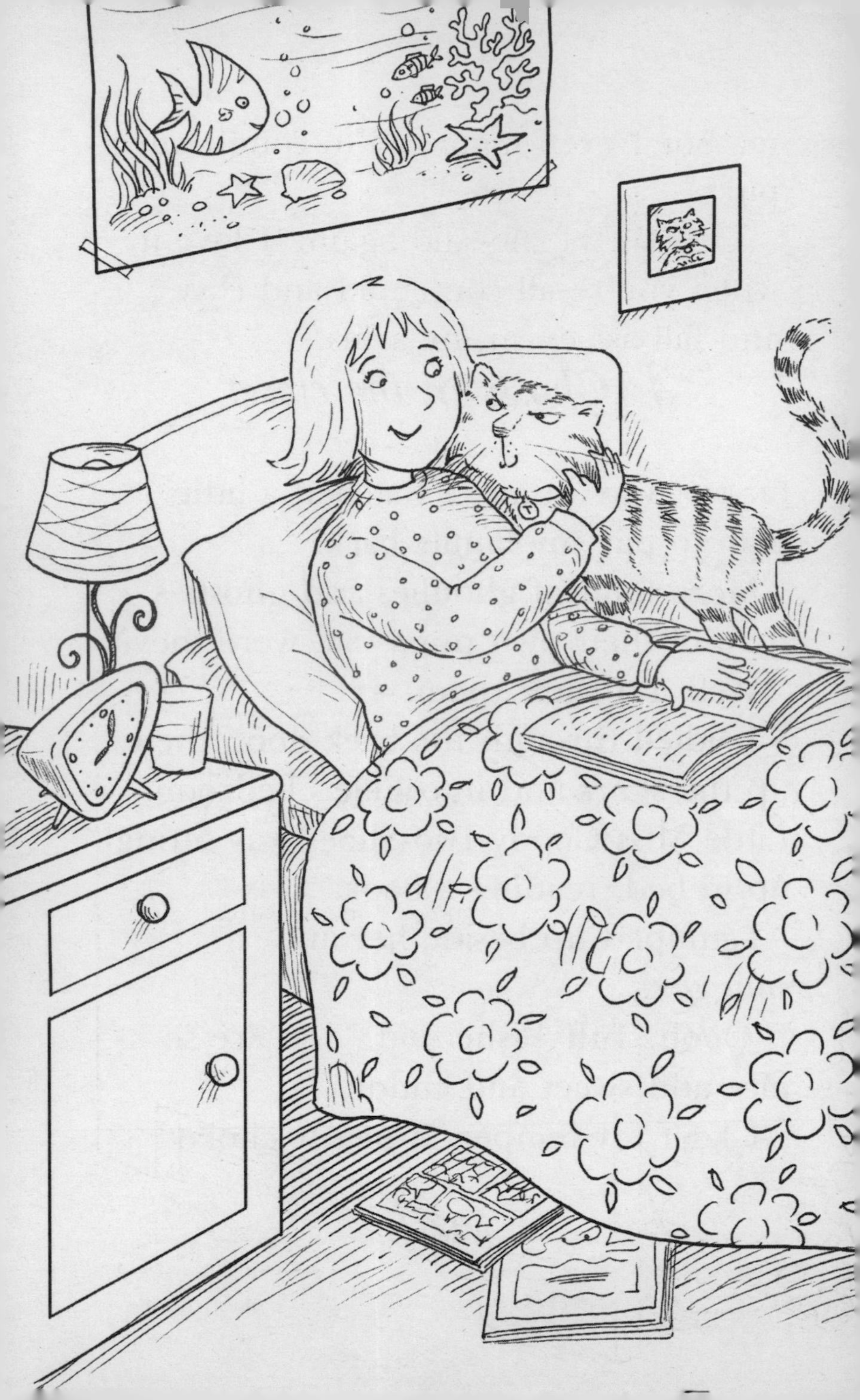

me but I even managed to cough out a
purr.

'Oh, Tuffy,' she said again. 'I love it
when you're all contented and cosy,
and fall asleep in my arms.'

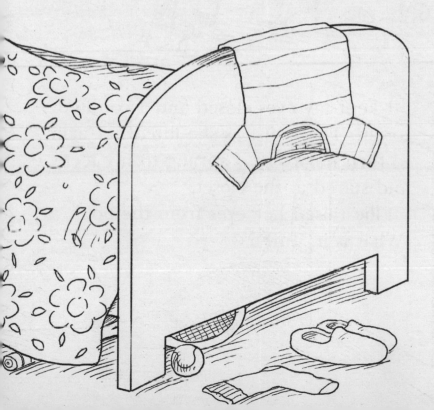

I kept my eyes closed and I counted
to ten. Then, just as she lifted her arm
to turn her page, I sprang to my feet
and stared at the closet.

Ellie raised her eyes from the book.
'What is it, Tuffy?'

I arched my back, and kept up the mad stare.

'Come on, Tuffy,' Ellie soothed. 'It's just the closet. The only things inside it are clothes and shoes.'

I gave her a quick 'don't you believe it' blink, and made my hair shoot up on end.

Now she was getting nervous. 'Tuffy?'

She slid out of bed and went towards the closet.

'*Yoooooowwwwwwwwlllllll!*'

It was the clearest message not to go a single step closer. You didn't have to be a cat to understand: *Whatever you do, don't open that closet door!*

Terrified, Ellie fled downstairs.

I took a break. Then, when she came up again a few minutes later, holding her parents' hands, I sprang back into

'Terrified Cat Staring At Ghosts In The Closet' mode.

You could tell from the look on Ellie's father's face that she had dragged the two of them away from something rather good on telly. He gave the most perfunctory glance around the room, then glowered at me.

I kept up the arched back and the stiffened fur, and stared at the closet.

Ellie's mother slid the closet door open. She pushed the clothes hanging from the rail to one side and peered in. 'Nothing strange in here.'

'Check the other side,' begged Ellie. (She was really scared.)

Ellie's mother checked the other side. 'Nothing.'

'Check both sides at once,' insisted Ellie. So under her orders Mr Grumpy-Wumpy poked his head in on one side

and Mrs A-Whole-Lot-Nicer poked her head in on the other, and they flapped all the clothes about.

'Ellie, there's nothing unusual in here.'

I gathered myself up, did a frantic little 'I am *terrified*' dance and spat at the closet.

Ellie burst into tears and shouted angrily, 'Well, *Tuffy* doesn't seem to think there's nothing in there! And animals are *famous* for seeing ghosts.'

'Because they're stupid,' Ellie's father said, still glaring at me.

Oh, very friendly. So I spat again, taking good care to make it land on his trousers.

Ellie's mother could see that, at this

rate, we would be up all night. 'You'd better come and sleep with me,' she said to Ellie. 'And Dad can go in the spare bed.'

Ha, ha. I spend a lot of time on that

spare bed. But I can curl up. I wouldn't care to sleep in it if I was long and thin like him. It's just Lump City, that old bed.

He knew it too. On his way out, he gave me a pretty mean look. I put on a snooty air and tried to show him by the way I stalked past that that is what you get for choosing not to hold a party for your own precious pussy.

Ghosts in the closet and lumps in the bed. That's what you get. And serves you right.

5: When poodles fly

THE COUNTDOWN BEGAN. If you're a friend of mine, it was a countdown to my birthday. If you are not, it was a countdown to Halloween.

I did a good bit of sulking.

Okay, okay! So I did more than sulk. I brought in dead things while they were eating lunch, and shed hairs over their pillow cases, and scratched great holes in all their precious carpets.

All in all, I had an excellent week.

Finally the big day came. Early that afternoon, the family drove off to get the stuff for their party. I'd seen the

35

list. *Food. Scary decorations. Halloween masks . . .* I'd scoured it from top to bottom several times but hadn't seen the very important words '*A present for Tuffy*'. And that could not have been because they didn't have the money, because when they came back with armfuls of expensive shopping I saw they'd splashed out on something that wasn't even on the list.

A floodlight for the front of the house.

He's not the world's best handyman. So when I saw him going to the tool cupboard to find the things he needed to wire it up, I thought it wiser to leave.

It was a bad time to be out and about. Just before dark. Dogs everywhere, all being taken out for the last proper walk before their families sit

down to supper. That's the worst thing
about dogs. Everything they do makes
trouble for others. Think about it.
When they get bored with staying
home and doing all the stupid things

37

they do – 'Come!' 'Beg!' Fetch!' 'Down!'
– they have to make a nuisance of
themselves fussing and whimpering to
get their owners to take them out.

Me? I just stroll out of the door.

Dog owners have to find the lead, and then untangle it. They have to find a couple of plastic bags in case the dog leaves a mess. (Ugh! Ugh! Ugh! Ugh!) Half of the owners even have to stuff

their pockets with treats just to get the dog to the park and back.

Dogs hate it when we laugh at them. But, really! It's a bit pathetic to be that

size and not be trusted even to cross a road all by yourself. Or find your own way home.

Still, it was daft of me to get in that argument when I saw Mrs Pinkney dragging Buster away from the nastiest lamppost in town.

'Diddums still wearing his baby rein?' I couldn't help jeering.

Whoops! I hadn't noticed Buster's great-aunt Tilly coming the other way.

'Just watch it, Fatso,' she growled. 'Don't pick on Buster or I'll pick on you.'

I looked down my right side. Then I looked down my left. 'No,' I said. 'I can't see myself trembling with fright. But that may be because I think I have the edge on anyone being tugged around on a long piece of string.'

'You think you're so clever?' she

snarled. 'If cats are so wonderful, where are the guide cats for the blind? Why don't the police have sniffer cats?'

'Yeah!' Buster jeered. 'All you lot do is go around stalking songbirds.'

'Better than barking at them all day like a squirty little lame-brain.'

He lunged and, startled, Mrs Pinkney dropped the lead.

I took off like a rocket.

'You wait,' threatened Buster's great-aunt Tilly as I shot past her. 'Our gate isn't always properly shut. I'll get you one day.'

'When poodles fly!' I yowled back
from the safe side of the wall. But I
was glad that Tiger had put his paw
down about having no dogs at the
party.

6: Not long now

I DIDN'T FORGET to invite Misty.

'Yo, dude!' she yowled. 'A party! Excellent! That rocks.'

Then I remembered Muff and Puff. 'Why bother to call it a party?' they asked me when I told them. 'Isn't that what we do all the time? Stay out all night and make a noise?'

'You're not invited,' I reminded Pudge the terrier. 'No dogs at this party.'

'Oh, boo woofing hoo,' he jeered.

'Will there be games?' asked Fluffball.

'Only the usual,' I said. 'Hide in the

46

Hay Bale. Shred the Straw. Cry Mouse!
Oh, and we'll probably have races
round the rafters.'

Together we strolled along to the
barn. Up in the hay loft, Georgie was
ignoring the spiders' grumbling as he

scooped up their cobwebs and draped them around the rafters in attractive festoons. 'I'm going for a natural, no-frills look,' he explained to us. 'Folksy. Naive. And I am tending to stick with the earth tones.'

'Do you mean brown?' asked Fluffball.

Georgie gave her a stern look. 'Come on!' he scolded. 'Look around. We've a style rainbow here. Khaki and chestnut; oatmeal; toast, mushroom and rust;

biscuit; bran and tobacco leaf; coffee and fawn –'

We left him reeling off his precious shades of muddy brown and went to look at the food.

Snowball was standing proudly in front of a hay bale spread with delicious goodies. 'Most of it comes from KeenKost,' he explained. 'Today is their clear-out day. And I have laid my paws on some excellent pâté only a day past its date stamp.'

I peered into one of the tubs. 'Well, whisk my whiskers! Is this double cream?'

'Nothing's too good for the birthday boy!'

I peered over the edge. Below, the horses were shifting from hoof to hoof.

'Getting excited, guys and gals?' I asked them. 'Well, it's not long now!'

7: *Spooking the horses*

IT WAS A brilliant party. It absolutely *rocked*.

First we played Boomerangs.

Then we did races round the rafters. I chose Tiger's cousin Marmalade as my partner for the doubles because she looked as if she'd corner well. And I was right. We won our heat by a mile, and then we waltzed away with the main race.

We ate all the grub. Boy, was that tasty! Better than anything they were eating back at the Halloween party. And when we were all feeling totally

stuffed out and bloated, we played
Spook the Horses. That was a little
mean, considering that it was past their
bedtime. But it's a good laugh. All you
have to do is wait till the poor old
dears are nodding off in their stalls,

53

and then you drop on their big fat
bottoms from a great height.

No claws. That would be cheating.

They wake up, startled, and they
neigh.

Neeeeigh! Neeeeeeeigh!

Five points for a single neigh. Ten for a double. Two extra points for any hoof clattering. And there's a bonus of ten if all the horse's hooves lift off the ground at the same time.

Great game!

The problem is we played it for much too long, and woke the farmer. She wasn't in the world's best mood when she came stomping into the barn in her boots and pyjamas.

We all laid low while she went down the line of horses in their stalls, patting and soothing. 'Hey, fellas? What's the problem? Are you all right, Dolly? What's all the fretting about?'

She glanced up at the loft. I thought she might climb the ladder and see the mess we'd left on our makeshift hay-bale table. But we were lucky. She just stood listening.

Not hard enough, if you want my opinion. If she'd been doing a proper job, she would have heard those tiny footfalls across the straw.

She would have turned, to see what we saw.

Buster and two of his rough little terrier mates creeping in through the stable door that she'd left open.

And by the time the farmer turned to leave the barn, they were as safely hidden behind the wheelbarrow as we were up there in the loft.

8: Here comes Ugly Club

HATE ME FOREVER if you like, but I'm still going to say it.

I hope your mum and dad keep you inside on Halloween!

And *if* you manage to nag them long enough to let you go out to show your brand-new monster mask to all the neighbours, I hope they've taught you how to shut a gate. The kids in our town must have let out every dog for miles around while they were Trick or Treating. By the time we cats sneaked out of the barn to get away from Buster and the terriers, the place was

swarming with dogs of every shape and
size and description, all running up to
join the fray and all barking their
heads off.

'Hey, pussies! Don't even bother
trying to escape! We're going to eat
you up and spit you out as fur balls!'

'Quick, Rusty! Head them off!'

'Grrrrr!'

'Max! Wolfie! Don't let the wee sleekit beasties get away over that wall!'

I tell you, if I had known that I was going to have to leg it all the way back into town at that speed, I would never have finished up that tub of pâté.

Or the last three fish heads.

Or that cream puff.

We took the shortcuts, over the walls those four-footed slugs can't jump. Most of my party guests peeled off as we shot past their homes.

'Night, Tuff! Thanks for an ace bash!'

'Volcanic night, Tuff! See you around!'

'Roll on same time next year!'

By the time we turned the corner into our street, there were only me, Bella and Tiger left.

Bella glanced back over her shoulder to check for dogs. 'I think we lost the dandruffy little creeps.'

'Way, way behind,' agreed Tiger. We skidded to a halt in front of my house and stared. The place was humming – bursting with party people. We could see them all through the windows,

holding their glasses high, and talking
and laughing.

We watched for a moment, and then
I asked the other two, 'What do you
reckon? There's bound to be *someone*

in there who's allergic to cats. We could have a good laugh. Shall we creep in?'

But they were no longer looking at the people inside the house. Tiger and Bella were staring at the big bright

circle thrown on the house wall by our brand-new floodlight.

'Groovy!' said Bella.

'Seriously cool,' Tiger agreed.

I looked at the gleaming ring of light.

'It is good, isn't it?' I found myself admitting.

'Hey!' Tiger said. 'We mustn't waste it. Let's play Guess the Shadow.'

'Me first!' insisted Bella.

Standing beside the little floodlight set in the grass, she stuck out her tail and curled it round, till just the tip was sticking up at the top.

Sure enough, inside the circle of light on the wall of our house fell an enormous shadow.

'A Mister Softee ice cream?' guessed Tiger.

'Dog doodoo!' I suggested.

I won that round. Then it was Tiger's turn. He stepped in front of the floodlight and curled himself into a perfect oval. When he was steady, he stuck the very tips of his paws out at the top.

Bella and I stared at the silhouette he'd made on the wall.

'A sack of coal?' suggested Bella.

'Two slugs having a race down a rubbish bag' was my guess.

I think we might have stood there

guessing all night. (It was an owl.) But just at that moment the hysterical barking and baying noise that had been getting closer and closer finally came round the corner.

'Oh, oh!' said Tiger, hastily
unravelling himself. 'Game over. Here
comes Ugly Club.'

'No, no,' I reassured him. 'None of
that pack of ratbags is fit enough to

jump over our fence. We're perfectly safe.'

Forget playing Guess the Shadow. Let's play Guess Who Was *Superwrong*.

Yes. That's right. Me.

Because that rattlesnake-eyed Alsatian who thinks she's such a star for winning gold cups at the Dog Agility Class swept over the fence, screeched to a halt, then, getting up on her hind legs, jammed her paw down on the gate latch.

And suddenly every dog in town was in our garden.

Ugly Club had arrived.

9: Terrifying Beast

OKAY, OKAY. so feed me worms all week.
The dogs got into the house.

How is that *my* fault? How was *I*
supposed to know that when I sprang
back like that, with my claws sticking
out and my hair up on end, this giant
shadow of me would appear on the
wall.

I didn't realize I would end up
looking quite so fierce.

And *huge*.

And scary.

I didn't know my shadow was going
to frighten all those wussie dogs *that*
much.

Nor was it my fault that they all
ended up running around in circles,
yelping and whining. Bella and Tiger
only leaned against the gate by *accident*.
They didn't know it was going to swing
shut, and trap the whole pack. (All
except Miss Dog Agility, of course, who
made it back over the fence and home

to her stupid collection of fancy gold cups.) As soon as the rest of them saw that they were trapped, they slunk on their bellies round and round our garden – a pack of wimperoonies, all

desperate for any way to escape from that Terrifying Beast that was so Fierce and Huge and obviously coming out of somewhere to get them.

Okay, so spank me. How was *I*

supposed to know that one of those
great lard-butted Labradors was going
to back up so hard against our front
door that it flew open.

In they all rushed, to get away from
the monster.
The whole pack.
Straight into the party.

There was some angry shouting, a good few screams and the ugly thump of overturned furniture. We heard a lot of breaking glass, and then the party guests began to tumble out of the house into the garden, to get away from the demented dogs.

I looked at Tiger and Bella. Tiger and Bella looked at me.

I glanced up at the silhouette. I had become a giant pussy cat.

Now that was simply *boring*.

'What do you reckon?' I asked the others. 'Party on, dudes?'

'Why not?' said Tiger. 'Once you're on a roll . . .'

'Absolutely,' agreed Bella. 'Go for it, Tuff. Command Performance!'

So I went for it.

10: The very best of shows

I DON'T THINK any group of people, ever, in the whole history of the world, can have been frightened so easily.

Of course, it helped that it was Halloween. What had Ellie's father called it? 'The time when everything evil and ugly and dangerous crawls out to stalk the land. A very suitable day indeed for Tuffy's birthday.'

Well, it was a very suitable day indeed for Tuffy's greatest performance.

Except, of course, that it was not day. It was night. Dark, with almost no moon. The trees were bending in the wind, and all those dogs howling and whining and whimpering made an excellent soundtrack.

So I stood in front of the little floodlight set in the lawn and I went for it. I clawed the air. I arched. I spat. I writhed. I bent my head sideways and gave a host of evil leers. I stood up on my back legs and scratched the air. I spun round. I bared my teeth.

My word, it was the very best of shows. Tiger and Bella kept up a soft, ethereal, other-worldly yowling that would have made my fur stand up on end if it had not been up on end already.

People and dogs spilled out of the door. They were all fighting one another like starved rats in a bag. It was the *perfect* moment, and down came the claws in my shadow like a

velociraptor snatching at prey.

Snatch!

Snatch!

Snatch!

Snatch!

The party guests screamed. Everyone
– people and dogs – took off in a
shower of sparks, shrieking hysterically.
There was much wailing and rolling of
eyes. There was a lot of banging of the
gate. There were a lot of terrified cries.
We heard them growing fainter down
the street.

Fainter and fainter.

Fainter.

Fainter, still.

In the end, there was silence.

Out over the heaps of flattened
sausages on sticks stepped Ellie and her
father. I leaped aside, but it was just a
shade too late. They'd spotted what I

80

was doing – turning my last ferocious velociraptor pounce into a final bow.

Mr No-Sense-Of-Humour didn't take it very well.

'You!'

Tiger and Bella don't much care for
the man when he's in one of his
tempers. They scuttled off home, fast.
I was left eyeing The Master.
He'd worked himself into a frightful

froth. He looked as if he'd like to take a cattle prod to me. He looked as if he'd rather like to tie me into a reef knot, and whirl me round and round his head.

'You vile, destructive little beast! You've *ruined* our party! Absolutely *ruined* it!'

I was about to give him the blink, turn on my paws and stroll off – after all, I'd had my supper – when Ellie turned on him.

'Don't you blame Tuffy! Don't you

see? All he was trying to do was scare off those nasty dogs who burst in after the food!'

She scooped me up and buried her face in my fur. 'Dear, kind, sweet, clever Tuffy. He saw the mess the dogs

were making of our house, and then remembered all about the ghosts in my closet.'

'There *are* no ghosts in your closet!' Ellie's father roared. 'There are no ghosts at all! And there are definitely none in your closet!'

'If *Tuffy* thinks there are, there are,' said Ellie. (I will say this for the poor noodle-brain. She really is loyal.) 'And if he thinks there aren't, there aren't.'

An *excellent* tip. I really hoped he would remember it. But, frankly, he didn't look as if he was in the mood to try to remember anything while he was cleaning up after the party. It took all night. In the end, Ellie and I went off to bed, of course. But I was woken several times by all the tinkling and muttering and cursing and banging as he swept up broken glasses and pulled the furniture the right way up to shove it back in place.

But, let's face it, Ellie's father has never had much thought for others. Selfish and inconsiderate, that's him.

At least, thanks to Ellie, I now have a good way of taking revenge on him whenever he's mean to me. What did she say? 'If Tuffy thinks that there's a ghost in the closet, then there is.' So if I feel like giving him a good night's sleep, I settle down on Ellie's bed and yawn and close my eyes. And so does she. Within a minute or two, she's fast asleep.

And, if I feel like paying him back for any of his petty meannesses (like having a party to celebrate Halloween instead of my birthday), I stare at the closet most uneasily, until Ellie hurries off to sleep in her mum's bed.

Then he gets sent along the hall to have a bad night in the Bed of Lumps.

And I feel great.